This book belongs to

_____

Clowning Around

Published by Advance Publishers
www.advance-publishers.com

Written by Annie Auerbach
Illustrated by Dean Kleven, John Raymond, and Yakovetic
Editorial development and management by Bumpy Slide Books
Illustrations produced by Disney Publishing Creative Development
Cover design by Deborah Boone

ISBN: 1-57973-021-3

It was opening night at the run-down Ritz Theatre in The City. Onstage, Slim was acting in a play. He was playing a prince.

Suddenly a lovely princess made her entrance—
and hung her cape on Slim's head! She thought he
was the coat rack!

Upset, Slim stormed off the stage.

After the show, the director said, "Slim, everyone keeps mistaking you for other things."

"I know," said Slim. "I hate it when that happens!"

The director continued, "I don't think you're built to be an actor. I'm sorry, but you're fired."

With a sigh, Slim followed the director to the door. They passed the snack bar, where Slim's friend Heimlich was working. Well, actually, he was eating . . . and eating . . . and eating.

"And you're fired, too!" the director cried.

"What do we do now?" Heimlich asked Slim as they stood outside.

"I'm not sure, but if we stick together, we'll be okay," Slim told him.

And so they set off to see what The City had in store for them.

As they wandered around The City that night, they passed a comedy club. Inside, a ladybug had just come onstage. As she was about to tell a joke, a fly in the audience shouted, "Hey, lady! I love that polka-dot dress!"

"I'm *not* a lady!" yelled the ladybug.
And he wasn't—he was a guy named Francis.
Unfortunately, after Francis's act was finished,
the owner of the club fired him. "Yelling at the
customers is just not funny," the owner explained.

Francis stormed out of the club—and bumped right into Slim and Heimlich!

"Pardon me, Ma'am," said Slim.

"Listen, you twig, I'm a Mister!" declared Francis.

"Are you having a bad day?" asked Heimlich.

Francis nodded. Then he calmed down and explained what had just happened.

"I think I know how you feel," Slim told him. "Our old boss didn't appreciate us either."

"What's your story?" Francis asked Heimlich.

"I got fired again," sighed Heimlich.

"Again?" asked Francis.

"Oh, yes. I've had all sorts of jobs," explained Heimlich. "But I just can't wait for the day I'll turn into a beautiful butterfly."

"With your appetite, you'll be the biggest butterfly ever!" teased Slim.

"And I thought I was the only comedian in this group!" joked Francis.

"I'm an *actor*, not a comedian," corrected Slim. "Oops! Sorry, stick," said Francis. "Hey, why don't we get a good night's sleep? Then tomorrow, we'll all go job hunting together."

The next morning, the three friends got an early
start. Almost immediately, they passed by a sign that
read "Auditions Today with the Great P.T. Flea."

They couldn't believe their luck! Francis thought
it might be his big chance. Slim imagined becoming
a famous actor. Heimlich just hoped there would
be food. The three friends hurried inside the tent.

"Hurry up!" called P.T. Flea as they entered.
"Time is money! And I don't have a lot of either!"

Francis auditioned first. "Why did the bee cross
the road?"

"I dunno, lady, why?" yelled P.T. Flea.

Francis continued, "To get to the other hive!" He laughed loudly at his own joke. Unfortunately, no one else did. Then Francis yelled out, "Hey, this is funny stuff! I'm a—"

"Next!" shouted P.T.

It was Slim's turn next. Heimlich was going to help with the audition by pretending to be a princess. Slim found a piece of cotton candy to use as a wig. He put it on Heimlich's head.

"Oh, princess, where are you?" began Slim.

But Heimlich didn't answer. He couldn't because his mouth was full of cotton candy!

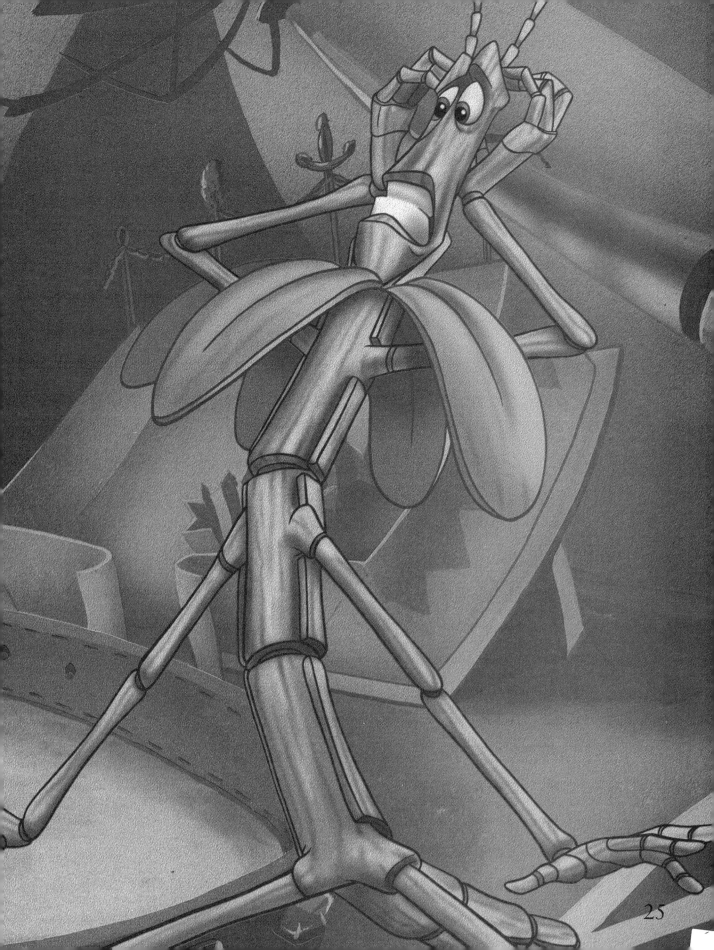

Francis knew he had to do something to help save
his friend's audition. He charged over to Heimlich.
"Give me that!" he cried as he tried to grab the candy.
"No! No! No!" shouted Heimlich. "I'm hungry!"

Francis and Heimlich played tug-of-war with
the candy. Finally it broke apart, sending Heimlich
backwards—where he landed on top of Slim!
"Bravo!" yelled the other performers, laughing
and clapping. They thought it was part of the act!

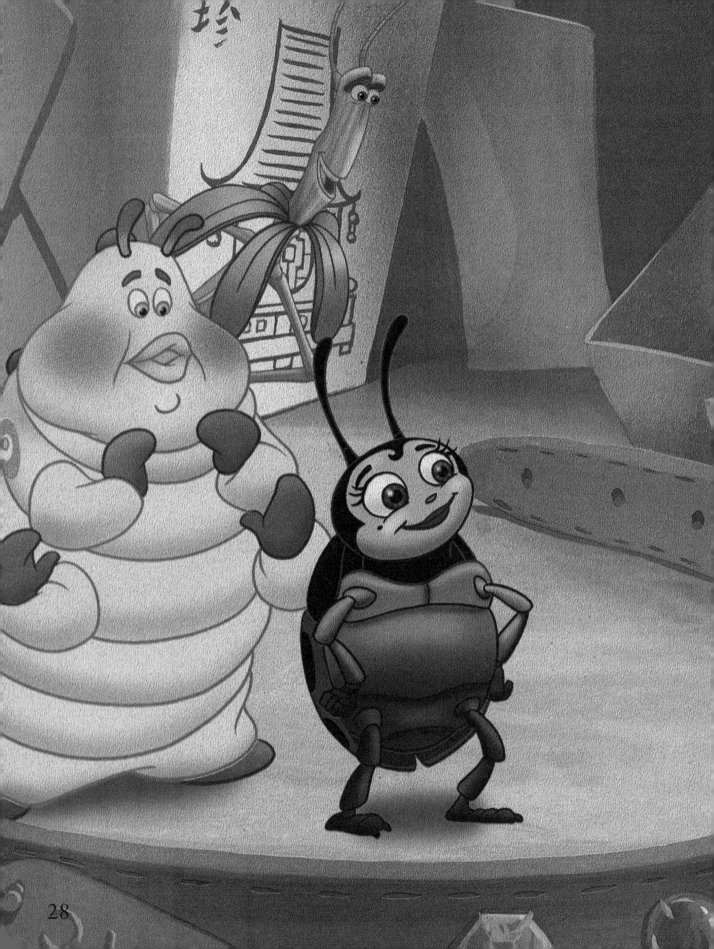

"You guys are horrible!" cried P.T., jumping up.
"But I think with practice, you could work your
way up to 'rotten'!"

"Does that mean we got the job?" asked Francis.

"Welcome to the P.T. Flea circus family," said P.T.
"Against my better judgment, you guys are my new
clown act. Rehearsals start tomorrow."

"Circus?" said Francis.

"Clowns?" said Slim.

They couldn't believe it! They didn't realize they had been auditioning for a circus!

"I can't be a clown," said Slim. "I'm a serious actor!"

"And there's no way I'm wearing makeup,"
insisted Francis.

But Heimlich started to think about all that
wonderful circus food—cotton candy, popcorn,
peanuts. His mouth began to water.

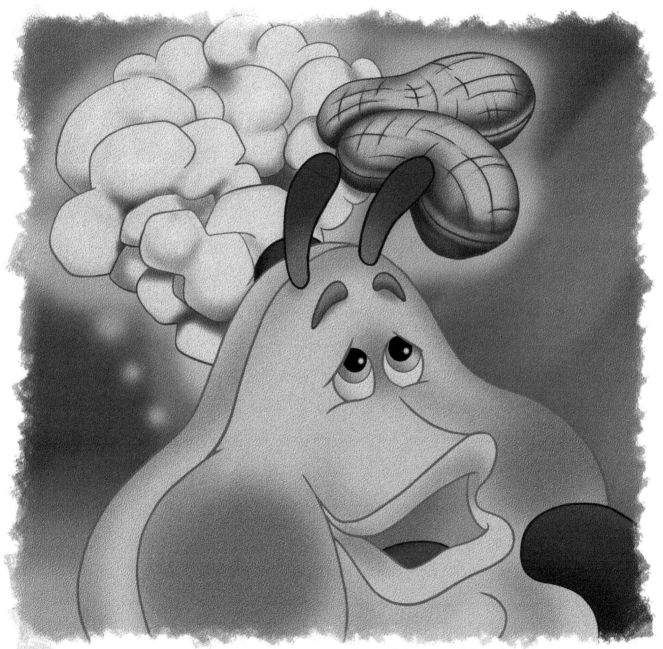

"What other choice do we have?" Heimlich said to the others.

"The caterpillar's right," said Francis. "And at least it's show business!"

Finally Slim agreed. "Well, it'll pay the rent,"
he said. "*And* we'll be able to work together."
Francis and Heimlich couldn't argue with that!

The other members of the circus did their best to
make the newcomers feel at home.

And during the next few weeks of rehearsals,
Heimlich, Slim, and Francis became good friends.

Now the performers waited nervously for the show to begin.

"Okay, everyone, break a leg!" said P.T.

"Ooh!" cried Heimlich. "That sounds painful! I have a lot of legs to break."

"It's just a saying!" snapped P.T. "Now let's get this show on the road!"

P.T. walked to the center ring and introduced the first act. Francis appeared, dressed in a hula skirt. But he sure wasn't happy about it.

Francis picked up a limbo stick that was actually Slim. Heimlich tried to squeeze his plump body underneath.

"Ooh, that tickles!" giggled Heimlich.

"Hurry up!" complained Slim.

Just then, Dim jumped on the eyedropper
cannon, launching Tuck and Roll. The pill bugs
flew through the air, heading straight for Francis!
"Aaagh!" the ladybug screamed.

Francis picked up Slim and swung him like a baseball bat. That ladybug hit both pill bugs right into Rosie's spider web. A double play!

Tuck and Roll bounced off the web. The other performers rushed to catch them—but crashed into one another instead!

P.T. pulled himself out from the bottom of the heap. The lights came up on the empty seats. P.T. looked around at the mess and sighed.

Lucky for him, tonight's performance was just for practice. The *real* show was tomorrow!

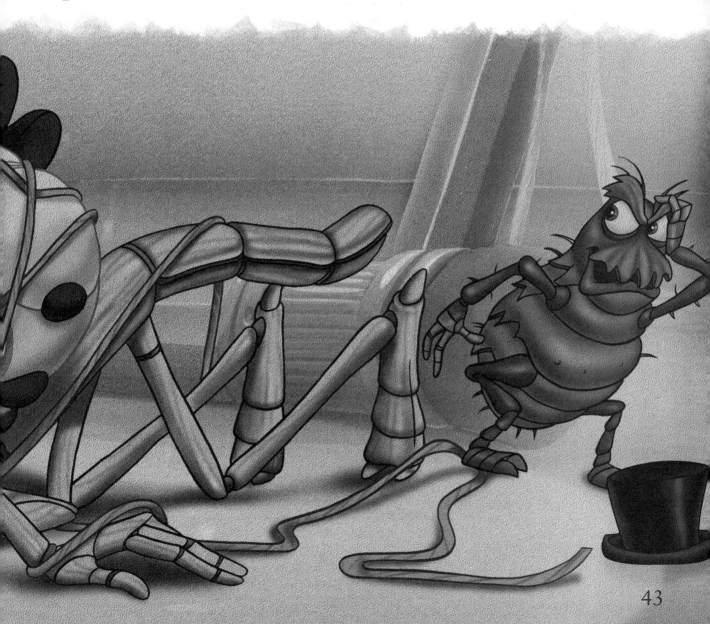

43

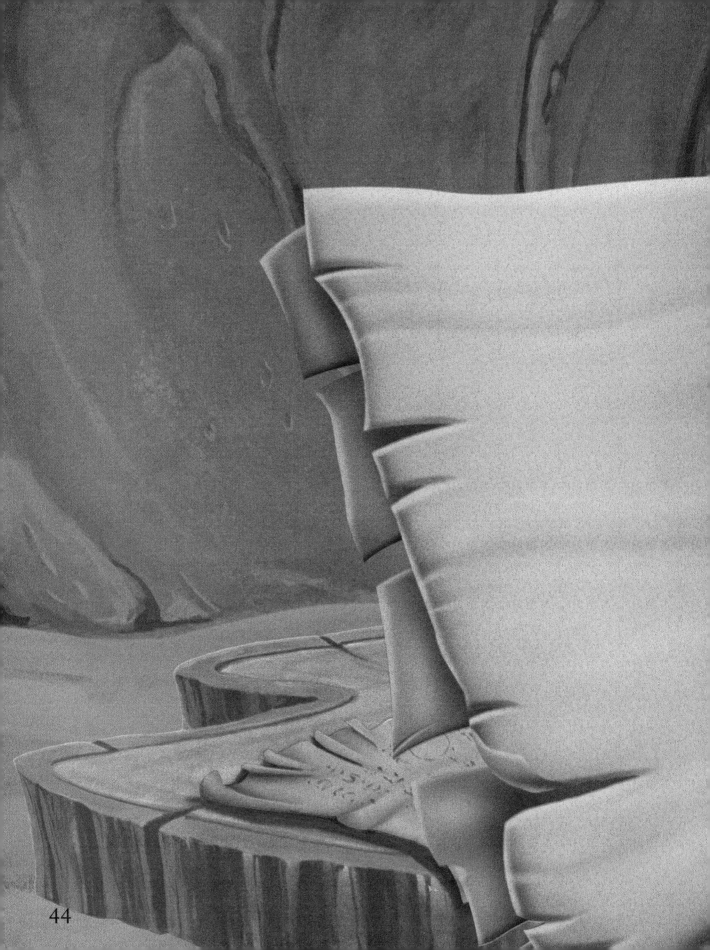

Dear Blueberry Journal,

Today Flik told us all about how bugs can look like other things.

Slim helped show us how. Slim is a walking stick. Walking sticks are bugs that are brown and shaped like sticks. That way, when they are walking on the bark or branches or twigs of trees, you can't see them at all. Neat!

There are also bugs that are green. When they sit on leaves, they are almost invisible. You can only see them if you look really, really hard.

Wait until Manny finds out he's not the only bug who knows how to do a disappearing act!

Till next time,
Dot